Cherish

Cherish

Ken Duncum

Victoria University Press

VICTORIA UNIVERSITY PRESS
Victoria University of Wellington
PO Box 600, Wellington

First published 2004

National Library of New Zealand Cataloguing-in-Publication Data

Duncum, Ken, 1959-
Cherish / Ken Duncum.
ISBN 0-86473-493-X
NZ822.3—dc 22

Printed by Astra Print, Wellington

First Performance

Cherish was first performed at Circa Theatre, Wellington, on 18 October 2003, with the following cast:

JESS	Luanne Gordon
TOM	Edwin Wright
MAEVE	Rachel House
WILLIAM	Bruce Phillips
ELIZA	Hariet Heron
	and Nikita-Maree Norris

Director	Katherine McRae
Set and Costume Designer	Sean Coyle
Lighting Designer	Jo Kilgour
Composer	Nic McGowan
Stage Manager	Rob Ormsby
Technical Operator	Amy Delahunty

Characters

Jess	30
Tom	30
Maeve	28
William	51
Eliza	3–4

Acknowledgements

Cherish was commissioned by Circa Theatre through the Michael Hirschfeld Memorial Writing Award.

The play was shaped through readings, workshops (funded by Playmarket and Circa Theatre) and the invaluable input of the following actors, director and dramaturg: Rachel House, Luanne Gordon, Edwin Wright, Bruce Phillips, Katherine McRae, David O'Donnell, Angie Meiklejohn, Richard Edge, Phil Grieve, Tandi Wright, Eleanor Aitken, Mark Amery, Emily Regtien, Claire Waldron, Jason Whyte, Conrad Newport, Michele Amas.

Act One

Lights down. Images are screened directly onto the set—still photo scenes from Scarlett's birthday party showing Scarlett (five) and Eliza (three) along with other kids and Jess, Tom and Maeve. Lights up on—

Scene 1: Jess and Maeve's house

Evening. Post-birthday. JESS *on the couch eating grapes—*TOM's *head in her lap, ear pressed to her belly.*

TOM: So what else did they say?
JESS: I've told you.
TOM: That's all they said?

> JESS *gives him a look.* TOM *hears something.*

My God. Listen to that borborygmi.
JESS: Beg pardon?
TOM: It's like a concrete mixer in there.

> TOM *imitates—with increasing exaggeration—her rumbling stomach, progressing to creaking doors, cats yowling and other barnyard sound effects.* JESS *grins, pushing him away.*

JESS: I'm getting up. I'd better make a start with all this—[party mess]
TOM: Nooo!
JESS: It's too early to feel anything.
TOM, *diving into her lap*: Please . . .
JESS: If you're going to be rude about my insides . . .
TOM: It's lovely—it's lovely in there—*Nosing into her*:—let me back in—I want to go back—all warm, floating round on a lilo . . .
JESS: That's me, is it—the lilo?
TOM: You're the most pneumatic, the most comfortable—

7

Sincerely:—the most beautiful and perfect mother my kids could ever wish for.

> JESS *puts her finger to his lips and he kisses it. He turns to kiss her belly.*

Right, Horace?

> *He lies on his back again, ear pressed to her.* JESS *strokes his hair. Pause.*

What else did they say?

JESS: Umm . . . 'I'm just going to squeeze some of this lubricant onto your tummy—it might feel a little cold.'

> *She shoots him an ironic glance.*

TOM: I'll just look at the scan.

> TOM *picks up an ultrasound scan and gazes at it.*

JESS: What did you say? Bor-bor—?

TOM: Ig-me. Stomach noises. It's one of William's words.

> *Beat.* JESS *stares into space.*

JESS: Where do you think William'll whisk you off to this time?

TOM: Whisk me off?

JESS: Well, it was Phuket after Eliza.

TOM: I can't go anywhere. He knows that. What would the Plunket Nurse think if she comes round and I'm in Phuket? *He looks at her.* You could, though.

JESS: What?

TOM: Go somewhere. After the baby.

JESS: No . . .

TOM: William would give you the money. I'll ask him if you like.

JESS: No. *Warning*: Don't.

> *Beat.*

Though you could tell him about the automatic payment.

> TOM *looks at her.*

TOM: Might be hard for you. At first.

Jess doesn't want to talk about it.

Jess: It's all too far away.

Tom: Six months. It's like looking at something through the wrong end of a telescope. *To her belly*: Hurry up!

> Maeve *enters.* Tom *makes no effort to move from his prime position with* Jess—*instead relishes it.* Maeve *circles them through what follows.*

Jess: Did they go down?

Maeve: Eventually. It was like they were both on speed. Sugared to the max.

Tom: Birthdays come but once a year.

> Maeve *starts to pick up, looking for something.*

Jess: Leave that. I said I'd do it.

Tom: God, what an appalling sex life birthdays must have. Only being able to come once a year.

> *As* Maeve *continues—*

Jess: Sit down. There's some wine left.

Maeve: I will in a minute.

Tom: Imagine if you're the 29th of February—that's once every four years—you might as well become a monk.

Maeve, *to* Jess: What if the school's started swimming? We'd better put Scarlett's togs in her bag in case.

Tom, *to* Jess: Remember that guy you met at orientation one year who was going to become a monk—said it was his last weekend before entering the seminary?

Jess, *pointedly*: No. I don't remember.

Tom: I like the sound of that word. Seminary. Makes me think of somewhere all white and glistening.

> Jess *catches* Maeve's *hand.*

Jess: Sit down. I'll clean—you sit.

> Jess *looks pointedly at* Tom.

Tom: I'll get you that glass of wine.

> *He goes off.* Maeve *sits beside* Jess *on the couch.*

JESS: All right?

MAEVE: Tired. *She looks at* JESS. So should you be.

JESS: Second trimester. Think I'll build a deck. *She puts her hand on* MAEVE'*s*. The kids all had a great time.

> MAEVE *smiles at her, then slides a hand down the cushions of the couch.*

MAEVE: Seen jingle-ball?

JESS: Is that what the crying was about?

> MAEVE *shakes her head, then admits reluctantly—*

MAEVE: Scarlett's got a scratch—under her eye.

JESS, *carefully*: She OK?

MAEVE: They were both beside themselves. It's ridiculous—all that cake and lollies. On top of the Kindergarten farewell . . .

JESS: I thought you were going to cut Eliza's nails.

MAEVE: I did. *She hesitates.* It was a colouring pencil.

> TOM *comes back in with the half-full bottle of wine and a couple of glasses. As he pours one for* MAEVE—

TOM: You'll love this, Maeve. This guy I was talking about—the almost-monk—gave Jess the whole story. There he was—on the brink—facing a lifetime of devotion to God and no sex. So naturally Jess does the decent thing—

JESS: Are you being deliberately annoying?

TOM: Several times, if memory serves. Drained him dry enough to keep his mind on the job for at least a month.

MAEVE: I really don't want to hear this.

JESS: Tom—

TOM: But this is the point! Then he turned out to be from Teachers College—majoring in Phys Ed! I mean, what an outrageous abuse of trust! No wonder you decided to stick with women. *He leans in mischievously.* Except—didn't you have him again a month later?

JESS: I liked the way he could isolate his muscle groups.

> *Annoyed,* MAEVE *jumps up.* JESS *catches her hand.*

Maeve!

WILLIAM, *off*: Hello! Only me!

Jess: For God's sake—it was years ago!
Tom: Everyone has to experiment with heterosexuality!

>   William *enters.*

William: I beg your pardon?
Tom: Finally—he arrives.
William: To find you experimenting with heterosexuality?
Tom: Well, you've been ages.
William: Everyone's entitled to their day in court. Though
>   someone should tell them they can't all have the same day.
Tom: Perhaps you should.

>   *They kiss.*

William: Where's the birthday girl?
Tom: Where do you think?
William: I'll just pop up—

>   William *heads for the stairs.*

Maeve: I've just—[put them down]

>   *But* William*'s gone.*

Maeve: If he gets them up again . . .
Tom: You know what he's like. William's not a big kid at heart,
>   he's a big kid all over. You should see the new sound system—
>   I'm not even going to tell you what it cost. But can I get him
>   to finish the baby's room?

>   *Unnoticed, talk of the baby's room strikes a chill through*
>   Jess.

Maeve: Are you sure that side of the house—?
Tom: We're going to do that whole cloud thing on the walls. It'll
>   be like flying.
Maeve: It just seems so far away from your room.
Tom: William snores! I don't want that waking up Horace every
>   five minutes. Mind you—*He gestures to* Jess*'s stomach.*—with
>   the racket going on in there, it'd probably be a relief.
Jess: Don't call him that. It that.
Tom: Horace?
Jess: You start it as a joke—then it sticks.

TOM: All righty then—lend me your names book.
JESS: It's Maeve's.
MAEVE: On the shelf in the kitchen, I think.

>   *She goes to look.*

TOM: I'll slip it into William's briefcase—he'll read it thinking it's
>   a class action with a long list of appellants.

>   JESS *doesn't respond.*

TOM: As far as he knows—I was there for the scan, OK?
JESS, *distracted*: Mmmm.
TOM: You didn't mind, did you? It's just that Jamie was only in
>   town for the day . . .
JESS: It's fine.

>   MAEVE *comes back in with the book.*

MAEVE: I hear giggling.

>   WILLIAM *comes down. They look at him accusingly.*

WILLIAM: They were awake!

>   *He's holding a little kindergarten-craft bird made from egg
>   carton and coloured feathers.*

Scarlett's birthday and she gives me a present—the darling.

>   MAEVE *sits beside* JESS *and opens the book. As they share a
>   moment, flicking through marked names in the well-thumbed
>   pages,* WILLIAM *spots the handicam and picks it up.*

Did you get it all? Every balloon, every kiddy-vomit and
expression of crazed excitement?
TOM: I did—[but]
WILLIAM, *reacting to his tone*: What?
TOM: I forgot the thingy.
WILLIAM: What thingy?
TOM: The lens thingy.
WILLIAM: The cap? It won't let you film with that on!
TOM: Seemed to. It was whirring away. Then—right at the end I
>   looked—and I'd had it on the whole time.
WILLIAM, *bewailing as he rewinds, viewing to check*: That's

impossible! That's why I got it. It's foolproof. Even you couldn't— *He sees the party footage.* —Oho. Very funny.

MAEVE, *reading to* JESS: 'Horace. Light of the sun. Keeper of the hours—'

JESS, *reading over her shoulder*: 'Worthy to be beheld.'

WILLIAM, *viewing*: Look at Miss Scarlett with her presents—like Queen of the May! *Aside*: She's absolutely agog with excitement about school. Though a teensy upset at having to turn up for her first day with a disfigured face.

TOM: What?

MAEVE: It's a scratch! That's all!

JESS: I'd better check her. *She gets up.* To TOM *as she goes*: AP . . .

TOM: Oh—better take this up.

He pulls the jingle-ball—a child's toy made of plush with a bell inside—from his pocket and tosses it to JESS.

MAEVE, *exasperated*: Is that where it was?

JESS *exits.*

What sort of word is 'disfigured'?

WILLIAM, *engrossed in the video display*: Oh—here's the cake!

TOM: Keep your eye on that Brendan kid with the pointy head . . .

WILLIAM, *witnessing comic disaster*: Oh . . . oh . . . oh no . . . ! *Noticing something*: What's that you're giving them, Tom? You know that stuff is full of food colouring. They'll be hyperactive—up all night!

TOM: Give some to you if it keeps you up all night.

WILLIAM, *lowering the handicam*: You haven't got a clue—honestly.

TOM: There's plenty of Maeve's carrot sticks left—have one and shut up.

TOM *feeds* WILLIAM *a carrot stick.*

Oh—there's some kind of problem with the money. The automatic payment.

WILLIAM, *to* MAEVE: That bloody bank! *Back to* TOM: How did the games go? Little Liza keep up?

TOM: Slightly sticky when she wouldn't pass the parcel.

WILLIAM: Wonderful! Is that on here?

TOM: Every tension-packed second.

WILLIAM: Excellent carrot, Maeve. Mine went all woody. What are you putting on them?

MAEVE: The cat comes over from next door.

> TOM *snorts.*

WILLIAM: Charming. Still want those cuttings from my daphne? Then behave yourself.

> MAEVE *has poured the last of the wine for* WILLIAM. *She hands him the glass as he's reaching for his chequebook.*

WILLIAM: I'll write you a cheque . . .

MAEVE, *uncomfortable*: No. No, it's fine.

WILLIAM: I'll get straight onto the bank tomorrow. Savage someone. *He puts the chequebook away.* Well—my day was murderous. How about everyone else's?

> As JESS *comes back in*—

TOM: Jess's day was 'sound'.

WILLIAM: Safe and sound? Sound of wind and limb?

> MAEVE *is looking at* JESS.

JESS, *to* MAEVE: She's fine.

TOM: Extremely highly sound. Wasn't it, Jess?

JESS: Ultra sound.

WILLIAM: Oh, my God . . . the scan! *To* TOM. Why didn't you tell me it was today?

TOM: I told you.

WILLIAM: He never tells me anything.

TOM: I told you!

WILLIAM: Well, don't keep me in suspense—is it a he, a she, a them?

TOM: You're going to have to hold on to your suspenders a while longer. They couldn't be sure of the gender yet.

> MAEVE *darts a surprised glance at* JESS, *which* JESS *avoids.*

> But—*He produces the ultrasound scan with a flourish.*—he's got my head!

> WILLIAM *takes the scan and examines it.*

WILLIAM: Ah yes—swollen—and full of amniotic fluid.

> WILLIAM *joins* JESS *and* MAEVE. *The four parents assemble for a moment round the scan, gazing at it.* WILLIAM *kisses* JESS *on the forehead.*

Clever girl.

> JESS *touches the scan with her fingertips.* TOM *breaks the circle by swiping the picture to gloat over it.*

TOM: I don't care what sex he is. As long as he's healthy, whole, ten fingers, ten toes—and prodigiously well hung.

WILLIAM: As if. We all know you're only good for girls. *He winks at* JESS *and* MAEVE. What else did they say?

JESS, *taking the scan from* TOM: Don't you start. Tom's been asking non-stop.

> *Uh-oh.* JESS *realises she's let the cat out of the bag as* WILLIAM *looks at* TOM.

WILLIAM: You weren't there?

TOM, *caught out*: Something came up.

WILLIAM: You've been ticking off the days.

TOM: Forgot I had a deadline. That proposal for Learning Media. But I'll be there for the next one. *To* JESS, *trying to divert attention.* I will so be there that you probably won't need to go. *He sticks out his stomach.* They can just scan me and my hysterical sympathetic pregnancy!

> WILLIAM *feels humiliated in front of* MAEVE *and* JESS.

WILLIAM, *smiling thinly*: Let's get you home before your waters burst.

TOM: Well, Mummy and Mummy—time for Daddy and Daddy to go.

> WILLIAM *kisses* JESS *and* MAEVE.

WILLIAM, *covering*: Five years! Frightening! I'll call tomorrow for a full report on Scarlett's first day in our world-beating education system. *He shoots a look at* TOM. Come on, breeder.

> WILLIAM *goes.*

Tom, *kissing* Jess: Thank you so much for blowing my cover. Remind me to kill you.

> *He grabs the scan but* Jess *holds onto it.*

Jess: Tom—
Tom: I want to gaze at it.
Jess: I thought I'd use it to start a book—like Maeve and I did for Scarlett and Eliza.
Tom: Honey, I've already started it.

> Tom *slips the scan from* Jess*'s fingers, and kisses* Maeve.

Ciao bella. Am I picking up Liza-with-a-z from kindy tomorrow afternoon?
Maeve: I'm working there tomorrow so—[you don't need to]
Tom: I'll see you there—and we can all go up to the school together. So exciting!

> *He follows* William. Jess *stands, lost.* Maeve *watches her.*

Jess, *covering*: I suppose there's dishes for Africa. Toss you for them.
Maeve: You're not tossing me anywhere.
Jess: Wanna bet?

> Jess *grabs* Maeve, *trying to lift her up. They struggle, laughing, turn it into their version of rock 'n' roll dancing.* Maeve *picks her moment.*

Maeve: You didn't tell Tom about the scan?

> Jess *doesn't reply.*

Why?
Jess, *breaking away*: I feel like I should be doing something . . .
Maeve: What about the next one? When Tom's right there beside you and they say 'Of course we told you last time it's a boy'?

> Jess *looks stricken, fear overtaking her—fear she's been holding back.*

Hey . . .

> Maeve *comes to her, leans her forehead against* Jess*'s.*

JESS: Cloud-pattern walls. Like being in mid-air. What's comforting about that?

MAEVE: We knew there'd be a few strange days.

JESS: All that blue and white. It's cold!

Beat.

MAEVE: It's real now. That's all. Not just an idea.

JESS *shakes her head.*

Forget the dishes. Into bed with a cup of tea.

MAEVE *heads for the door.*

JESS: Could you do it, Maeve?

MAEVE *stops.*

Could you do it if you were me?

Pause. MAEVE *feels the ground opening underneath her.*

MAEVE: Don't ask me that.

JESS: I tried to tell Tom. I knew how he'd be—grinning, lighting up like he does—running round texting everyone. 'It's a boy.'

Beat.

I wasn't expecting the scan to be . . . It was so much clearer than any of Scarlett's. He moved. I saw his heart beating.

JESS *looks at* MAEVE.

Could you, Maeve?

MAEVE: Why are you asking me that now? All the times we talked it through—you never asked me.

JESS: I suppose I knew what you'd say.

MAEVE: And now you want me to say it?

JESS *stares at her, frightened, on the brink.*

JESS: I can't *see* any of it any more. I hear Tom saying things. It's like—looking at something through the wrong end of a telescope. No. That's not really happening. I'm not really going there. I'm not just handing over my baby. There's going to be no cloud patterns. No other house. No.

She looks at MAEVE *in panic.*

Maeve?

> MAEVE *sees her distress. As much as she wants this not to be happening—and not now—*MAEVE *can't deny* JESS *the support she's asking for.*

MAEVE: No. I couldn't do it. Not when I think how I felt carrying Eliza. I never knew how you could say you could.

> JESS *stares at her, crumbling.*

JESS: What am I going to do?

> MAEVE *comes to her, holds her.*

MAEVE: Tom'll just have to see. He'll have to understand.

> *Over* JESS's *shoulder the look on* MAEVE's *face is much less assured than her words . . . Lights down.*

Inter-scene images: images from the scan of the baby.

Scene 2: Jess's studio

Afternoon—a week later. Sunlight streams through the wide windows of the studio at the top of the house. TOM *is reading over some work, editing as he goes, scribbling here and there. He's in the middle of telling a funny story to* JESS, *who's offstage.*

TOM: All right, I laughed. I know it probably wasn't the right thing to do. But William has never danced! Even when I managed to get him in a club. And there he was—like a one-man Woodstock—music up loud—totally oblivious—totally uncoordinated—flinging himself round the lounge. Honestly, Jess—if you'd been there . . .

> JESS *enters with a large illustration, mounted on cardboard, turned towards her.*

JESS: I suppose you were out seeing someone?

TOM: . . . It's possible.

> *He catches her look.*

It was nothing. It never is—you know that.

JESS: Does William?

TOM: William doesn't need to know. What the eye doesn't see the heart doesn't grieve over.

JESS: What you must put him through sometimes . . .

TOM: What?

JESS: Last week.

TOM: Missing the scan?

JESS: He must have suspected.

TOM: It wasn't mentioned again. Doesn't cross his mind. Anyway— what about what he puts me through? I was the one who came home to be confronted by the sight of the Manic Marionette! It's seared into my memory.

JESS, *getting down to business*: OK . . .

TOM: OK.

JESS: Promise you won't panic?

TOM: I promise—no such thing. Show.

> JESS *turns the illustration round.* TOM *gazes at it.*

Oh, honey.

JESS: What?

TOM: It's fantastic.

JESS: Really?

TOM: You're going to have to find another partner. I can't write to this standard.

JESS: Stop joking.

TOM, *putting down his work*: No, that's it. I'm not equipped to work with genius. I haven't got the temperament.

JESS: Don't be so hard on yourself. It's a picture book—

TOM/JESS, *a familiar mantra*: Who's going to read the words?

> *Beat.*

TOM: Having said that—*He picks up his work.*—I'm thinking of changing the dog's name. To Quentin.

JESS: Changing his name?

TOM: Rags is a bit trad, don't you think?

JESS: You can't do that.

TOM: We haven't done the lettering yet. His name's not anywhere in the pictures. I've done it, see?

> *He holds up the edited work.*

JESS: I've drawn Rags the dog. That's what I've drawn. If he was called Quentin I'd have done him differently.

TOM: How?

JESS: Just differently.

TOM: Sort of . . . Quentin-ly?

JESS: Yes. Actually.

TOM: OK . . .

JESS: You can't just change things like that, Tom.

TOM: Only trying to aspire to your level of brilliance.

JESS: Sorry.

TOM: No problem. *He scribbles.* See. There he is—back again. *He holds up the re-corrected work as if it is the character.* Rags the dog. Bouncy, bouncy, bouncy.

> *JESS props the illustration up.*

JESS: You honestly like it?

TOM: I love it.

> *They look at it.*

Sure about the face on the beach ball, are we?

JESS: Too scary?

TOM: Too . . . too . . .

JESS: Too-too?

TOM: You think so?

JESS: I could take it off.

TOM: Could you?

> *JESS nods.*

Let's try that.

JESS: The rest is just sketches so far. *She picks up a handful of neatly cut strips.* Or was sketches.

TOM: Eliza?

JESS: I left them downstairs for five minutes.

TOM: Precocious, see? William Burroughs didn't discover the cut-up technique till he was in his 30s.

JESS: It seems to keep her happy for hours. In her own little world.

Which reminds TOM—

TOM: Have we ever had Eliza's hearing tested?

JESS, *with an ironic look*: 'We'? Her hearing's fine. She only hears what she wants to.

TOM: It's always worked for me. Are you swimming this afternoon? *He checks his watch.* Whoops. I've got the painter coming at two. *He stands.* Would that were true! He's going to size the walls of the baby's room. I'm told he's a tremendous size—though I haven't had the opportunity to find out for myself.

TOM *is on his way out*—JESS *knows she has to say something.*

JESS: There's no hurry, is there? For the baby's room.

TOM: Can't have you popping Horace out without a home to go to. Sorry! *To her belly*: Whatever your name is.

JESS: Baby wouldn't be coming straight to you. Anyway.

TOM *stops.*

TOM: 'Anyway'?

JESS: I'll be breast feeding.

TOM: I can bring bub over during the day. Then you can express some I can keep in the fridge.

JESS: I'd never be able to express enough.

TOM: Once you got into the swing of it.

JESS: It'd starve.

TOM: I suppose we could go straight on the bottle.

He sees her expression.

Don't give me that La Leche League look. Plenty of women do it to stop their nipples cracking so badly their piercings fall out.

JESS: Tom—I've got to bring the baby home here.

TOM: And I what—come and stay for a few weeks?

JESS: You could. There's only the couch.

TOM: We've got plenty of room. There you go—you come stay with us.

JESS: I can't do that.
TOM: Why not?
JESS: There's Scarlett to think about. And Eliza.
TOM: Bring them too.
JESS: Don't be silly, Tom—this is their home.

>   TOM *looks at* JESS.

TOM, *gently*: Don't you think, if you feed you might get . . . too
attached?
JESS: More attached than I am now?

>   *Beat.*

I'm not going round with swollen leaking tits—
TOM: Express.
JESS: You express!
TOM: Express myself?

>   *He throws a modern dance shape.* JESS *laughs. He keeps it
>   up, cavorting about. She starts to cry.* TOM *comes over, puts
>   his arm round her.*

TOM: We'll be all right. All of us.
JESS: Don't be angry with me.
TOM: I'm not angry with you.

>   *She looks up at him, takes his hand, takes a breath . . .*

>   *Blackout.*

Inter-scene images: half-painted clouds on blue sky.

Scene 3: Café

Later the same day. Ambient café sound. Lights up on WILLIAM *and*
TOM *in mid-conversation at a table.* WILLIAM's *just said, 'Well—
that's that'.*

TOM: What do you mean?

WILLIAM: What do you mean, what do I mean?

TOM: You get it, right? You understand?

WILLIAM: Jess is not keen on you taking the baby.

TOM: On us taking the baby. *He corrects himself*: On us having the baby. We're not taking it.

WILLIAM: Yes. And that's what Jess has said. We're not taking the baby.

TOM: I can't believe you!

WILLIAM: So I get it, yes? I understand.

TOM: What the hell do you mean by 'that's that'? I feel like I've been hit by a truck! I tell you what's happened—

WILLIAM: You call me in the middle of a meeting, tell me there's a terrible emergency—

TOM:—and all you can say is 'Well, that's that'!

> *Beat.*

WILLIAM: I'm sorry. I'm upset. I shouldn't have said it.

> TOM *looks at* WILLIAM. *He reaches across the table.* WILLIAM *takes his hand.*

I hate to see you hurt.

TOM: Then tell me that is not that. Tell me that is something else. That is it! That is outrageous! That is unjust! Give me another that.

> WILLIAM *looks at him.*

WILLIAM: That is sad.

> TOM *stares at him.*

TOM: We're going to fight it.

WILLIAM: I'll talk to them.

TOM: She's not going to get away with it!

WILLIAM: Away with what? This isn't a frozen chicken she's stuffed up her jersey at New World—this is a baby!

TOM: My baby!

WILLIAM: Somewhat your baby, yes.

TOM: No! My baby! Scarlett and Eliza were their babies—this one's mine!

WILLIAM *pinches the bridge of his nose as if he's getting a headache.*

That was the deal! That is the deal!

WILLIAM: Ah yes—'the deal'.

TOM: Yes, I know—if we'd put it on paper, drawn it up as a contract—

WILLIAM: That wouldn't make the slightest difference. Not if it was sworn on the Bible and signed in blood.

TOM: What's the matter with you?

WILLIAM: As I told you at the time, a baby in utero—[doesn't belong to anyone]

TOM: This affects you too!

WILLIAM: Really, Tom? And you've just noticed, have you?

They stare at each other.

I'll talk to them.

TOM: I just—want your support. I need you to help me.

WILLIAM: We knew something like this might happen. We did discuss it.

TOM: Jess promised. Look what I've done for her—for both of them. She can't just go and change her mind.

WILLIAM: It's not her mind that's changed.

TOM: She's got Scarlett—Maeve's got Eliza. I did it—twice.

WILLIAM: Normal mathematics doesn't work here—

TOM: Don't talk down to me!

WILLIAM: She's the mother.

TOM: Oh—the great holy mother—!

WILLIAM: Yes, actually. Yes! Have a look round at the world, Tom—there's a difference!

Lights down.

Inter-scene images: Jess, Scarlett, Eliza and Maeve all holding hands.

Scene 4: Jess and Maeve's house

That evening. JESS *and* MAEVE *tensely waiting.*

JESS: I feel sick.

> *Beat.*

It's like being called to the headmaster's office. This is our home!

> JESS *gets up restlessly.*

I'm going to make the lunches.
MAEVE: I heard the car.
JESS: When?
MAEVE: Five minutes ago.
WILLIAM, *off*: Only me!

> WILLIAM *enters with a plastic bag of cuttings.*

Sweetheart.

> *He kisses* JESS.

Maeve.

> *He kisses* MAEVE, *then proffers the bag.*

I brought those cuttings.

> MAEVE *takes them.*

WILLIAM: Stick them in the ground—up against the fence—they'll go like there's no tomorrow.
JESS: Where's Tom?
WILLIAM: I sent him to the dairy for something. Don't overwater, it hates the hose, gets a kind of grey powdery mildewy-mould thing. *He sits down.* That payment coming through all right?
JESS, *distracted*: Sorry?
WILLIAM: I was asking if the payment's working.
MAEVE: Fine. Thanks.
JESS: The dairy?
WILLIAM: I said, Tom pop down to the dairy for something. He said, what? I said, anything. Absolutely anything. As long as you walk. And it's quite far away.

Jess: I'm sorry you had to be bothered, William.
William: No bother.

He smiles at them.

Jess: Would you like something?

She's halfway up.

William: Why don't you two tell me what it's about?

Jess *sits back down.*

Maeve: Tom's told you, hasn't he?
William: He garbled something. You know him. Something about where the baby's going after it's born. Isn't it? Once it's been bodily towelled off—all that blood and stuff that looks like earwax. Once it's been weighed and fingers and toes pronounced present and counted for. Whose gaff it heads for next. Nuestra casa o vuestra casa? Bit of a ruck forming over who does those crucial first midnight feeds. Parents from all corners of the field joining the rolling maul waving their bottles and breasts.

He whistles.

Scrum down on the 22. Introduce a bit of order. Yes? The referee's blown his whistle. That's me now. Is it?

Jess*'s nerve collapses.*

Jess, *to* Maeve: I can't do this.
William: So Tom mentioned.
Maeve: It's about where the baby goes. Full stop.
William: Ah.
Jess, *distressed*: I'm sorry, William. Truly.
William: So what appears to be the problem?
Maeve: Isn't that obvious?
William: Feelings? Coming up. Bubbling to the surface.
Maeve: That's a little patronising.
William: I don't mean it to be. I'm just trying to—establish the nature of the catastrophe. Jess?
Jess: I feel so stupid! *She looks at* William. You know I'd never hurt Tom. I couldn't do that.

WILLIAM: Strange. He was doing a good impersonation of being hurt this afternoon.

> JESS *ducks her head.* MAEVE *sees nothing is going to come from her.*

MAEVE: Jess can't just hand the baby over to Tom and you. She can't do it.

WILLIAM: After all that's been said? This has been coming for years.

JESS: I know!

MAEVE: It's different.

WILLIAM: When you come to it. Yes. I can see that.

> *Beat.*

What about a delay?

> JESS *looks at him.*

Some time with the baby before it comes to us. Six months? A year?

> JESS *looks at* MAEVE.

JESS: We could—[say that]

MAEVE, *to* WILLIAM: No.

> *That single word resounds.*

Still to WILLIAM: You know as well as I do what would happen.

JESS: Tom can have as much access as he wants. When the baby's old enough he can come to you for weekends.

WILLIAM: He can visit.

JESS: Of course.

WILLIAM: And Tom can visit him here.

JESS: And you.

WILLIAM: Just like we do already with Scarlett and Eliza.

JESS: Yes.

WILLIAM: Just like that.

JESS: More. If that's what you want.

WILLIAM: I'm not sure I can speak for what 'we' want. I could hazard a guess that Tom wants his son. I take it—from all this unbridled use of the masculine pronoun—it is a boy.

Their silence is affirmation.

And what I want at this particular point is not to be playing some cut-rate King Solomon.

JESS: I'm sorry.

MAEVE: Good. Since it's not your decision, anyway.

> *That hangs in the air.* TOM *comes in. He can immediately see what's going on. Or not going on. He flips* WILLIAM *a small package.*

TOM: Candy cigarettes.

WILLIAM: My favourite.

TOM: Well?

> *No answer. From any of them.*

TOM: Jess—see sense.

JESS: I am. I have. Now you have to.

WILLIAM, *to* TOM: Congratulations. It's a boy.

> TOM *looks at* JESS.

JESS: Tom, I love you. But I can't do it. I can't.

TOM: We don't want this to go to court.

WILLIAM/JESS: Court?

TOM: That's what we're trying to avoid.

WILLIAM: Hold hard Sir Harry—nobody's talking about court.

MAEVE: You don't need to, do you? You're a lawyer.

WILLIAM: There's no case to take to court.

TOM: We made an agreement. I've done my part.

WILLIAM: Where are you thinking of going? Small claims?

JESS, *to* TOM: You can't be serious.

WILLIAM: He's not serious.

TOM: What?

MAEVE: We're not scared of you.

WILLIAM: We're not here to do anything other than discuss the situation.

MAEVE: For now.

TOM: What did you think we'd do?

JESS: I hoped you'd understand.

TOM: You've got my son.

JESS: No!

She stands.

My son.

She exits. Beat. MAEVE *stands.*

MAEVE: Just go.

She exits. TOM *and* WILLIAM *look at each other.*

WILLIAM: Candy cigarette?

Lights down.

Inter-scene images: candy cigarettes package—image turning into strips.

Scene 5: Jess's Studio

Afternoon, a week later. MAEVE *is on the portable phone.*

MAEVE: So she's allowed to be angry and I'm not?

There is a thumping on the wall behind her which comes and goes in a maddening remorseless manner.

What do you expect from the kid of a couple of dykes—is that what she said?

The thumping continues as MAEVE *shifts position to hear better.*

Well, it's what she's thinking. Bloody KKK mothers.

Beat.

Karori, Kelburn and Khandallah.

Beat.

Her boy gets a couple of scratches—all right, a bite. I'll keep an eye on her, Sally.

Beat.

I know I'm supposed to be there for all of them—I know that!

Beat.

If you're thinking of banning Eliza, you can forget about me working there! Well that's how it sounded!

The thumping is louder.

Look, I've got to go.

She hangs up, agitated.

Eliza! Stop kicking the wall!

Jess comes in.

JESS: What are you doing in here?
MAEVE, *holding up the phone*: It was quieter.
JESS, *suspicious*: Who was it?
MAEVE: Sally. Kindy stuff.

JESS relaxes.

What did you think—I was calling a lawyer?
JESS: You said you wouldn't.
MAEVE: I didn't say I wouldn't ask around. *She takes out a card.* Perry Traynor.

JESS doesn't look at the card.

JESS: We don't need a lawyer.
MAEVE: It wouldn't hurt to talk to him. He's won heaps of cases in the Family Court.
JESS: It's not going to come to that.
MAEVE: Still think Tom'll just get over it?
JESS: He bounces back. That's what I used to call him at Varsity— Rubber Band Boy. A couple of nights clubbing and he'll be back on top of his world.

The thumping . . .

Scarlett said Eliza was in trouble.

MAEVE: She got overexcited this afternoon. I put her down for a nap—but she's too hyped.

JESS: She under the bed or behind the chair?

> *They regard each other—and right now* JESS *is the only person who could get a smile out of* MAEVE. MAEVE *smiles.*

MAEVE: Chair.

> JESS *turns.*

Leave her. She'll be all right.

> JESS *looks like she's going to go to Eliza anyway—but the thumping stops.* JESS *and* MAEVE *look at each other—and relax.*

JESS: What did Sally want? Was it about extending your hours?

> MAEVE *shakes her head.*

I thought they were going to by now?

MAEVE: That makes two of us.

JESS: Oh well—never mind.

MAEVE: Never mind?

> *She looks at* JESS.

MAEVE: We can't keep relying on money from William and Tom.

JESS: It's for the girls. And the baby.

MAEVE: And us. We live on it.

JESS: We both work.

MAEVE: We're busy all day—but kindy and working on your book doesn't pay the rent on this house. They know that.

JESS: They wouldn't cut off the payments.

MAEVE: They shouldn't have to. We should.

JESS: They've been paying for five years—

MAEVE: He has. William.

JESS: Whatever. They're not going to just take that away. And why should we?

MAEVE: It makes us vulnerable.

JESS: You're so . . . pessimistic about everything. We've told them. Tom knows things aren't going to turn out the way he planned. That doesn't mean everyone has to start being awful to each other.

MAEVE: You've stopped him seeing the kids.

JESS: I haven't!

MAEVE: You told him not to come round.

JESS: Not if he's going to get angry every time—start making threats. That sort of atmosphere's not good for the girls.

>   *Beat.*

Tom just needs to—accept things. When he does—

MAEVE: Life can go on—with their baby and their money?

>   JESS *looks at her.* MAEVE *looks down.* JESS *comes across to her—rubs her back.*

JESS: It's over now. We can get on with being a family. The five of us.

>   *She puts* MAEVE's *hand on her belly.* MAEVE *looks at it, then at the room.*

MAEVE: The sun really floods in here in the afternoon.

JESS: That's what makes it such a great studio—the light.

MAEVE: This is where you did it, isn't it? You and Tom. You said you wouldn't use our bed.

JESS: We didn't.

MAEVE: You'd do some work together, then what—round it off?

JESS: I suppose.

MAEVE: It's private. You can leave the curtains open—there's no one to see. Must have been nice. I bet you made sure it was nice.

>   JESS *is silent.*

I wouldn't let the girls come upstairs. I'd get them home and we'd just sit down there.

JESS: Why?

MAEVE: Afraid they'd see something. That I'd come up here and see you—the two of you—asleep in the sun. Because you did, didn't you—you lay together afterwards.

JESS: I just wanted this baby—and Scarlett—to come from something warm and loving.

MAEVE: We made love. When I got pregnant with Eliza. You were there with me when I did it. That meant something to me.

JESS: I know.

Maeve: Not to you?

Jess: I wanted something . . .

Maeve: What? Natural?

Jess: More—human.

Maeve: What does that make me?

Jess: I didn't want you fucking me with a turkey baster!

> *Beat.*

I don't know why you're asking all this now. You were the one who didn't want to know the details.

Maeve: You and Tom—you've got jokes I don't get and secrets I know nothing about. People see you together and think you're lovers.

Jess: We do. Love each other.

Maeve: I imagine you here, making love, and it's like this house belongs to the two of you. You might as well be in our bed.

Jess: Maeve—

Maeve: How it's supposed to be. Mother, father, kids. All happy together.

Jess: You're being silly.

> Maeve *looks at* Jess.

Maeve: Sometimes I think I don't know who you are, Jess. You've had men, you've had women . . .

Jess: Had. But I *have* you.

> *She puts her arm round* Maeve. Maeve *looks up almost fearfully at* Jess.

Maeve: Did you enjoy it? Sleeping with Tom? Having sex with him?

> Jess *looks at* Maeve.

Jess: What I enjoy—is you.

> Jess *and* Maeve *kiss. The thumping of Eliza kicking the wall starts again. Lights down.*

Inter-scene images: Jess and Tom making love on a makeshift bed on the floor of the sunlit studio.

Scene 6: William and Tom's house

Evening. WILLIAM *is putting his feet up with a glass of wine, listening to the Rolling Stones. He fiddles with the toy bird Scarlett gave him.* TOM *comes in.*

TOM: What are you doing here?
WILLIAM, *in an Eccles voice*: Everybody got to be somewhere.

> WILLIAM *uses the remote to pause the music.*

TOM: You're home early.
WILLIAM: It has been known to happen.
TOM: Did you do it today?
WILLIAM: Come here, Tom.
TOM: You come here. Did you cancel the money?
WILLIAM: I want to show you something.
TOM: Thanks, Mister, but I've seen it.

> WILLIAM *flashes a brochure.*

TOM *is suspicious.* What?
WILLIAM: Just look.

> TOM *takes the brochure.*

TOM: Portugal.
WILLIAM: The Algarve.
TOM: What's going to happen if I open this?
WILLIAM: Dangerous. You might fall in love. You might find yourself transported to some warm Iberian afternoon in a little hilltop town.

> TOM *holds the brochure over* WILLIAM *and opens it. Tickets fall out which* WILLIAM *catches.*

Oh—what's this?
TOM: You didn't do it, did you?
WILLIAM: Look at the dates. Four weeks, Tom. Four weeks!
TOM: Yes, that should be enough time for me to forget. I'll come back all bronzed with only a vague idea of what was worrying me. Oh yes—a baby.
WILLIAM: You'll see things differently. I know you will. Like Bali.
TOM: Bali?

WILLIAM: We both felt better after a week there.

TOM: For fuck sake—our cat died—it's a little different!

> *Beat.*

WILLIAM: You're determined to be a shit about this, aren't you?

TOM: Just cut them off, William. Cut the payment.

WILLIAM: It wouldn't make any difference if I did.

TOM: Try it!

WILLIAM: It would just hurt the girls. And turn it into some sort of vendetta that you—or I—couldn't get back from.

TOM: You're supposed to support me!

WILLIAM: I do support you!

TOM: They're using Scarlett and Eliza—keeping them away from me! What leverage have I got?

WILLIAM: That's what I'm saying—you're on a hiding to nothing. You'll only make things worse.

TOM: You never wanted that room finished. You never believed.

WILLIAM, *lifting the tickets*: Do you know what I had to do to clear this time?

TOM: I don't want to be taken away, to be taken out of myself. I want a life that's complete, that's rounded. I want to be a father to my son. I want what's mine!

> WILLIAM *cocks an eyebrow and uses the remote to turn the music back on—It's 'You Can't Always Get What You Want'.*

I don't give a shit what the Beatles have got to say about it.

WILLIAM: It's not the Beatles!

TOM: Whatever!

> TOM *grabs the remote and turns the music off.*

You could help. You could cut off their money, put pressure on them. You could start legal proceedings—you could do it in your tea break.

WILLIAM: How many times, Tom? One: there's no legal entity till the baby's born. Two: when that happens—because the two of you aren't married or living together—Jess will be its sole legal guardian.

TOM: Make something up! Anything! Anything to show them that we're not going to just take this.

WILLIAM: Are you really that eager for heartbreak? Because that's what you're asking for.

> TOM *looks at him.*

I promise you. If you think you've lost something now, wait till you see the scorched earth that would be all that's left behind.

> TOM *is mute.*

Baby, come to Portugal. With me. I know it won't wipe any of it out, I never thought it would. It's just—you've got to laugh to keep from crying. Let's get out of here—where we can at least breathe.

> TOM *looks at him bitterly.*

TOM: Easy for you.

> WILLIAM *tightens.*

WILLIAM: Easy for me?

> *He suddenly throws the brochure and tickets at* TOM.

When has any of this ever been easy for me?

> TOM *is surprised and stunned by* WILLIAM*'s outburst.*

Don't you think—when you used to go on about how desperate you were for children, that I felt . . . I love you. I would do so much for you. I do do so much for you. If anyone were to—give you children—don't you know how much I would want that to be me?

TOM: You've helped. You've made it possible—

WILLIAM: For you to have your children. Not our children.

TOM: The girls have always been like ours. You love them.

WILLIAM: Of course I love them. And whose fault is that?

TOM: Fault? That you've got kids in your life?

WILLIAM: They belong to Jess and Maeve. And you. You're in their blood—nothing can change that. But what am I? Some favourite Uncle—tolerated as long as I don't step too far out of line. And as long as I'm still the partner of their father. But the nose that runs in my family—well, it dries up here.

If I mingle my seed with your seed, all we get is two teaspoonsful instead of one. No baby—no special magical union, the bond between you and me made flesh. Just a bigger wet patch.

Tom: You can't just—[give up]

William: But that's the difference between me and you. I accepted that a long time ago. I'm gay. That means there's a couple of chapters of the Book of Life I don't get to read. I raged about that—then I came to terms with it. There are some things you can't have.

Tom: That's defeatist.

William: No—not if you don't consider it a defeat. The things you can't have—they define you, shape you. They belong to you. They're not an outrage to natural justice. They are nature. They're something to be cherished.

Tom: That's you all over.

William: Wanting something isn't the same as having a right to it. But you—you fight against that—nothing can stop you trying to grab the whole fruit bowl. That's why you fuck around behind my back.

Tom: What?—Who's been saying that?

William: I'm 51, Tom—I'm not senile!

>Tom *pouts.*

If I choose to ignore it, it's only in the hope that you might grow up some day. And in the meantime what alternative do I have—actually?

>Tom *burns with shame—and anger at being caught out—* >as William *presses his advantage.*

You know what I call it? The sushi approach to life. You think it's all laid out for you to pick this or pick that from the great big parade of what's on offer. And it's all fine—it doesn't matter as long as they're on separate plates. We're gay—so we can't have love and children on the same plate. But you can't even keep love and sex on the same plate.

Look at your life. Your partner is not the parent of your children, your children are half you, half someone you never wanted to unite with. You have all these halves floating around—but they don't add up to a whole!

Tom: There's probably a hundred thousand separated parents in this city—they're just the same as me.

William: Can you really not see the difference? Those are failures of love, tragedies, the death of dreams—but that's your definition of success, that's the highest you aspire to. Your ceiling is where other people begin.

Tom: How can you talk to me like I'm a cripple?

William: I've cursed myself for ever letting you start this. For indulging you, knowing it would end in tears. But how could I stop you? How could I be the one to say no? Now here we are. More or less where I expected to be. Except what I hate— what I really hate you for, Tom—is those days when your great idea jumped straight through your skin, when it burned so bright and shiny and naively that even I believed it too. *He exhales.* But now it's time to put it away. That great idea. With all the other things in the toy box.

> *He goes to put his arms round* Tom—Tom *fends him off at arm's length.*

Tom: You're so old. You make me sick.

> Tom *turns and walks out. Lights down.*

Inter-scene images: drawings by Scarlett and Eliza of Tom and William outside their house.

Scene 7: Jess and Maeve's house

Mid-morning. Maeve *comes in, having just answered the door.*

Maeve: I was just going out.

> Tom *follows her. He looks strained—but composed.* Maeve *is wary of him.*

Jess isn't here.

Tom: She's not hiding upstairs?

Maeve: If she was I wouldn't have let you in.

> Tom *looks round. He picks up the jingle-ball. A smile which is half pain crosses his face. He covers.*

Tom: Tickle your arse with a feather.

> Maeve *looks at him.*

Particularly nasty weather. It's one of William's.

> *Beat.*

I'd like to sit down.

> Maeve *nods.* Tom *sits. He gestures with the ball.*

How is she?

Maeve: Eliza's fine. Look—if you've come here for some sort of shouting match—

> Tom *shakes his head.*

Tom: Most people don't seem to think I've got anything to shout about. I don't have to ask where you stand on that.

Maeve: Where does William stand?

Tom: William takes the long view. I'm not surprised with a mother like his. Did you know she's 86? Iron in the soul, that woman. I think she expects to bury him. Funny thing is, he seems to expect it too. He's so—

Maeve: Pussy-whipped?

> Tom *looks at her.*

Tom: You don't like me much, do you?

Maeve: It's a bit late either way.

Tom: I wouldn't be the first person you'd choose to procreate with.

Maeve: I don't remember choosing—exactly.

Tom: Bit hard to cry rape—I wasn't even in the same room.

Maeve: Jess wanted Eliza and Scarlett to be sisters. You were already Scarlett's father.

Tom: Instant family—just cut out the middle man.

Maeve: You only did it so you'd get your own baby.

Tom: I did what you wanted. I gave you what you wanted.

Maeve: Look, Tom—I'm sorry it hasn't worked out for you. Honestly. But let's not pretend you bestowed on me the special gift of your sperm. You've always done your best to spread it round. You couldn't even make it to the baby's first scan because you were busy liberating a few million more.

Tom: Is that what this is about? That I'm not fit for the job? *He looks around.* Where's your certificate? When did you pass your proficiency test to be a parent?

Maeve: I've got to go out.

Tom: I'll wait for Jess.

Maeve: I don't know when she's due back.

Tom: I'll wait.

Maeve: What for?

Tom: You put Jess up to this, didn't you? You worked on her.
     What is it really about me you can't stand? Who I am? Or what I am?

Maeve: Gay?

Tom: A father. Scarlett's father. Eliza's father. The new baby's father.

Maeve: McDonald's father.

> Maeve *stops herself, not wanting to get into it.* Tom *challenges her.*

Tom: No, go on.

Maeve: All right Tom—McDonald's father. That's about your level. You've got a Daddy—then you come and play daddy over here. Take the girls out for treats, buy them clothes and play dress-ups, exciting sleepovers at your house. But then you're gone again. Because you're free to come and go. Because you've got a whole life to go to.

Tom: I want what you've got.

Maeve: You don't. You don't, because you'd have to lose something. There's no balance, do you understand? You've been reading too many magazines if you think there is. Women who've got it all. Well they haven't. If anything happens, if anything goes wrong, there's no choice. And if there's no choice there's no balance. When you've got kids anything outside of that is just flying a kite, you're let off the leash for a few minutes to imagine you've got a life. Until the next round of chickenpox or night terrors or mashed vegetables. And I don't care, I don't mind. But you couldn't stomach it.

> TOM *looks at her.*

And why should you? Why should you have to, why would you want to? You've got the best of both worlds. You've got it sweet, Tom. Accept it.

TOM: Would you?

MAEVE: I'm not a man.

> JESS *comes in with her swimming gear. She is surprised to see* TOM *there.*

JESS: Tom.

TOM: Hey up.

> JESS *hesitates a moment, then crosses to him and hugs him tightly. He hugs her back, his hands find her belly. They've both got tears in their eyes.*

Putting on a bit of beef, Jessie. What you got in there—a rugby ball?

JESS, *laughs*: Has Maeve offered you a coffee?

TOM: No. It's all right.

JESS: I've missed you so much.

TOM: I need to talk to you, Jess. Just the two of us.

> JESS *glances at* MAEVE, *realising this might not be the reconciliation she has thought.*

JESS: Maeve's fine.

TOM: She's going out.

MAEVE: I'm all right.

> TOM *looks at the two women.*

TOM: William says I should give it up, move on past it. He's refusing to help me. He says the law doesn't recognise a child in the womb as belonging to anyone but the mother. I wanted him to cut your money off. He wouldn't do it.

JESS: I know you're angry.

TOM: Where have I got to go, Jess? I've got nothing.

JESS: You've got us. You've got the kids. And William.

TOM: I want you to change your mind, Jess. Please.

> JESS *looks stricken, looks at* MAEVE.

You promised me, Jess.

JESS: Don't ask me.

TOM: All I can do is ask you. No threats.

JESS, *upset*: I don't want to hurt you.

TOM: Let's go back to Plan A. I've been looking forward to this, counting on this for five years. All right, not always seriously. But I can be, Jess. I will be.

> JESS *looks down.*

I'll be a good father. I promise.

> *The moment stretches out, until* MAEVE *can't stand it any longer.*

MAEVE, *to* JESS: Just tell him.

> JESS *looks up through tears at* TOM.

JESS: I can't, Tom. I made a mistake. I'm sorry.

> *Pause.* TOM *nods.*

TOM: I had to try. You understand?

> JESS *nods her head.*

I had to give us both a chance.

JESS: I'm so sorry.

> *She reaches for him—but he stands.*

It'll be fine, Tom—honestly—you'll see.

> TOM *takes out some folded papers.*

MAEVE: What's that?

> TOM *splits them, holds out a sheaf each to* JESS *and* MAEVE. JESS *reaches out but* MAEVE *stops her.*

TOM, *steely*: I got a lawyer of my own. Since William couldn't seem to muster the determination.

JESS: But you said—as long as the baby's in the womb—

TOM: These aren't about the baby. I'm claiming fifty:fifty shared custody of Scarlett—*He slaps a sheaf down.*—fifty:fifty custody of Eliza—*He slaps down the other.*—but the day the baby's born, Jess, you'll get another one of those. *He walks to the door.* You couldn't let me have one—now it's going to be three halves.

MAEVE: Get out! GET OUT!

> *She snatches the papers up and throws them at* TOM. *He shrugs, and exits.*

> MAEVE *is beside herself.*

No. No—

JESS, *stunned and vulnerable*: Maeve?

MAEVE, *turning on* JESS: NO!

Images of the legal papers are projected as the lights go down.

Act Two

Opening images: Ultrasound scans of the baby showing its development to the eight-month stage—interspersed with shots from a commuter train, ending on a suburban railway station.

Scene 8: Maeve and Jess's flat

Night. Four months later. JESS *and* MAEVE *are now living in a flat in Epuni. It is somewhat less salubrious than the house they've left.*

JESS and MAEVE *are on the couch, perfectly still, facing each other. Each has her hands together as if praying, fingers extended to just touch the other's fingers. They could be doing something new-agey, but they're not. They're playing slaps.* MAEVE'*s hands twitch and* JESS *jerks hers away. She moves her hands back and—at the touch—*MAEVE *slaps her.*

JESS: Ow! You're drunk.
MAEVE: Still faster.
JESS: That's what I mean. I wish I could drink.
MAEVE: Can't. I've drunk it all.

> *She giggles. Her hand whips out again.*

JESS: Ow! When's it my turn?
MAEVE: When you're quicker than me.
JESS: I'll never be quicker than you.
MAEVE: Then I guess—*Slap!*—we play until I'm tired of—*Slap!* -ing you.

> JESS *has jerked at each slap.*

JESS: I'll give the baby hiccups.
MAEVE: I'm tired.
JESS: You're falling down pissed.
MAEVE: Long as I can fall down on you.

She does, snuggling. They cuddle and kiss.

Big round Jess. Smooth heavy melon-breasts.

JESS: Little Maeve who's going to get squashed in a minute.

MAEVE *leans back, pulling* JESS *on top of her.*

MAEVE: Squash me.

They start to make love. JESS *puts a hand down to steady herself and feels something down the back of the couch. She pulls out a book.*

JESS: What's this? *She looks at it.* Did Perry drop this off? When?

MAEVE: Yesterday. It was outside the door when I came home. You were having your nap.

JESS: What's it doing down here?

MAEVE: Out of the way of Eliza Scissorhands.

JESS: You could have told me.

MAEVE: Forgot.

JESS: You never forget anything.

MAEVE: He's always round here.

JESS: You were the one who wanted him. The best lawyer for custody cases.

MAEVE: I know.

JESS *sits up, leafing through the book (the latest hot novel).*

JESS: He was telling me about this. He gets books off Amazon before they're published here.

MAEVE: I just don't know how we're going to pay him.

JESS: It'll be all right.

She finds a business card with something written on it at the front of the book. MAEVE *watches* JESS *smile as she reads a few sentences, then—*

He says 'Tell Maeve thanks for the tip.' What tip?

MAEVE: Background stuff. How will it be all right?

JESS: I don't know. Maybe we'll get costs. Perry says it's going to count against Tom that he wasn't interested in equal custody of the girls before—it'll look like he's doing it for revenge.

MAEVE: You don't need a law degree to work that out. He never wanted Eliza in the first place.

JESS: Of course he did.

MAEVE: Wake up, Jess—she was just a hoop he had to jump through to get his baby.

JESS: He loves her.

> *Beat.*

Perry says it usually comes down to a compromise—every second weekend or something.

MAEVE: No. No way.

JESS: They have to try to be fair to both parents.

MAEVE: What's fair got to do with it? This isn't a game. I need to know where my child is, what's going on—to be able to protect her. When I imagined having a child, it was always my child—there was no father.

JESS: After the one you had . . .

> *She puts a hand on* MAEVE's. *Beat.*

If it does come to a compromise—if that's the best we can do . . .

MAEVE: The best we can do is if Tom drops the case. So it never gets to court orders, or a legal debt we can't pay.

JESS: Perry doesn't think—

MAEVE: Perry, Perry, Perry . . . What does he care? Whatever happens he'll take his fee and go home to his nice house in Kelburn or wherever.

JESS: Oriental Bay. He's got an apartment. He goes swimming at the Freyberg every morning before work.

> JESS *broods.*

God, it seems like a hundred miles away. Another country.

MAEVE: You seem to be in town most of the time.

JESS: There's hardly any point in coming back once I've got Scarlett to school.

MAEVE: You can't be on your feet like that. Jess, you're nearly eight months. You can't put it off any longer. Scarlett's going to have to change schools.

JESS: She's lost her home—why should she lose her friends as well?

MAEVE: This is her home. We're her home.

JESS, *sighing*: At least I used to be able to go for a swim during the day. It gave me something to look forward to.

MAEVE: We couldn't afford it on top of the train fares.

JESS: It was my only luxury.

MAEVE: What about the luxury of not working?

JESS: What do you want me to do, go cleaning like you? I can hardly bend over.

MAEVE: No.

JESS: Or what? Waitressing? A plate in each hand and one on my belly?

MAEVE: I just want—a bit of reality about our situation. Jess, we had to move—you know we did.

JESS: I hate it here. It's so dark in this flat.

MAEVE: Townhouse.

JESS: What town?

MAEVE: If you weren't in Wellington all the time you might realise the Hutt's not so bad.

JESS: I dread the thought of bringing the baby home.

MAEVE, *for the nth time*: We need to be somewhere we can live within our means.

JESS: We had means. It was you who stopped the payment—not William.

MAEVE: They would have loved it if we'd kept taking their money. We'd get to court and they'd make us out to be a couple of two-faced money-grubbing bitches who wanted to have our cake and eat it too.

JESS: William's not like that. He's really concerned about us and the kids.

Pause.

MAEVE: If you were here more during the day—you could work on the book. Or start another one.

JESS: You said it wasn't worth it.

MAEVE: All I said was if you stack the price of materials up against what you've made from illustrating—well, it's not a lot. I didn't mean you shouldn't do it.

JESS: As a hobby?

MAEVE: Jess, I love your art. You know that.

JESS: I haven't got anywhere to work here.

MAEVE: Work on the table.

JESS: I need a space. A proper studio. Nothing's safe here. You can't put something down without it being cut to ribbons.

MAEVE: So it's Eliza's fault?

JESS: I didn't say that! I just want—

MAEVE: Tom to come back and say all is forgiven? Everything go back to how it was? Living in the city, William dispensing cash, you and Tom finishing the book? Everybody happy. Baby, book, house, swimming . . .

JESS: You try carrying this around 24/7. In the pool was the only time I got a rest from it.

MAEVE: Have more baths!

JESS: I would but you've turned the hot water cylinder down!

> MAEVE *takes a breath.*

MAEVE: Why are you clinging on to stuff that's gone, Jess? What are you waiting for?

JESS: You're happier here, aren't you? You think this is more real.

MAEVE: I'm doing the best for us I can.

JESS: This is how you've wanted us to live all along. Faces in the dirt but fiercely independent. Congratulations—you've finally got me.

MAEVE: Jess, this is where we live now. Scarlett has to go to school here.

> JESS *shakes her head stubbornly.*

Then what?

JESS: William's kept a sense of perspective. He'll see sense.

MAEVE: No he won't.

JESS: He'll make Tom see sense.

MAEVE: This is a war. By the time it's finished William's never going to want to see either of us again.

> JESS *looks at* MAEVE, *suddenly suspicious.*

JESS: What was this 'tip' you gave Perry?

MAEVE: Nobody's taking our kids. Nobody. You can't be civilised about that.

JESS: What did you tell him?

MAEVE: You want to blame me—you want to blame me for stopping the money, for everything. I'm out there every day with my head down other people's toilets working my arse off for us!

Jess: You've done something, Maeve.

Maeve: You want somebody to blame—look at whose bright idea this whole thing was.

Jess: Tell me what you've done.

Maeve: I wanted a sperm bank! But no—you had to have real siblings, the same father, you had to convince me it would bring us closer.

Jess: Is that what you wish? That you'd ignored me, gone to a sperm bank? So Tom couldn't touch you, so it'd just be me in court. Me, Scarlett and the baby.

Maeve: At least one of them would be safe.

> Jess *looks at her.*

Jess: Your one.

> *Lights down.*

Inter-scene images: Scarlett and Eliza's drawings, photos of Jess and Maeve walking apart, each with her daughter.

Scene 9: William and Tom's house

Late night. William *is sitting in the dark, music playing quietly, when* Tom *comes in.*

Tom: What are you still doing up?

> William *doesn't reply.*

Turn some lights on—it's like a brothel in a power cut.

> *He turns a light up. There's a half-drunk bottle of wine and a quarter-eaten Chinese takeaway in front of* William.

Yum. Little midnight feast is it?

He has a spoonful—it's cold. He pulls a face.

More like—what—8:30?

He swigs from the bottle to get the taste out of his mouth. WILLIAM *still hasn't spoken.* TOM *peels off his jacket, yawning.*

I'm shagged.

Beat.

Thought I might have caught you cavorting round the living room again. Come on, Daddy—let's see you do your dance.

Pause. TOM'*s pretty much run out of diversions.*

I'm sorry I didn't call. I got caught up.

Nothing.

You wouldn't believe what happened. After Peter giving me arseholes about dropping that creme brulee yesterday, tonight he only went and clouted this woman in the eye with a soup spoon. We were in hysterics. He tried to blame it on Eric changing the entrees at the last minute. I swear she'll have a black eye tomorrow. Then, right in the middle of everyone flapping round and her performing like she'd been shot, Eric's voice comes floating out of the kitchen, 'Oh, call the silly bitch an ambulance!'

He looks at WILLIAM. *Nothing.*

Fine. Be like that.

He goes to walk out, but turns.

I was working. All right, the restaurant's been shut for three hours. But sitting round after closing, having a few drinks, it's part of it. We need to chill out—what else is there to do, come home to bed? You're usually asleep with the light on.

Beat.

What? You think it's some sort of menage? Peter and Eric are both having me over the espresso machine?

Beat.

It's good to be able to—talk to people, you know? They seem to understand at least.

Beat.

You didn't want me getting a job. You don't want me working nights. We never see each other to talk—yada-yada-yada. Or is it actually that I'm doing this without you? Earning my own money to pay my own lawyer, when you thought I'd just throw a moody then get over it?

Beat.

Forget it. I'm shattered. I'm going to bed.

He walks out.

WILLIAM: I got a call today.

A moment, then TOM *comes back in, staring at* WILLIAM.

TOM: Well?

Beat.

No one's died? It's not your mother?

Beat.

William!

WILLIAM: They're looking into charges against me.

TOM *is baffled.*

TOM: What do you mean? At work? What's been going on?

WILLIAM: When I was seventeen. That charge. They're going to use it.

TOM: Who is?

WILLIAM: Who do you think?

Pause.

TOM: It was dropped.

WILLIAM: Makes no difference. They can bring it up.

TOM: It's ancient history. You were just a kid.

WILLIAM: No. He was a kid. I was an adult. In the eyes of the law.

Beat.

TOM: It's bullshit. It's bullshit. It's bluff.
WILLIAM: What did you tell them, Tom?

Beat.

They didn't just turn this up. They knew what they were looking for.
TOM: Nothing.
WILLIAM: Tom!
TOM: I might've said to Jess . . .

WILLIAM *looks at him.*

It was years ago—it just came out in conversation—I didn't know this would happen!
WILLIAM: Is there nothing, nothing between you and I that's stayed that way? That isn't out there for public consumption?
TOM: They can't be serious. It'll just come back on them. It's ridiculous!

WILLIAM *looks down.*

The judge'll throw it out. The charge was withdrawn. Innocent till proven guilty.
WILLIAM: That's beside the point. All they need to do is get the idea out there. Child molester.
TOM: He was fifteen!
WILLIAM: I know that! I know exactly what he was. Fifteen going on thirty-five—I might have been two years older but he was the experienced one. But that's not going to count for anything—that's not a sound bite. Sex with a minor—that's what sticks in the brain. Paedophile seeks custody of children.
TOM: What kind of scumbag lawyer would do that?
WILLIAM: A good one.
TOM: How can anyone stand up in court—
WILLIAM: He's hoping he won't need to.

TOM *looks at him blankly.*

It's called strategy, Tom. They wanted me to find out.
TOM: And drop the case? It's not you taking it to court—they must know that. You can't drop the case, only I can.

WILLIAM *looks at him.* TOM *gets it.*

Right.

TOM *turns away. Silence.*

WILLIAM: I don't have very much, Tom.
TOM, *raising a hand*: I don't want to hear it.
WILLIAM: Hear it! Listen to me! For once!

Beat.

I have my work. I have you. I have the girls—when and if all
this settles. I've got travel to look forward to in my holidays
and a bit of music in the evenings. That's me.
TOM: I didn't ask for this.
WILLIAM: Neither did I. But now the boot's on the other foot.
These people are going to hurt me, Tom. And I can't even
say I blame them.
TOM: Instead you blame me.
WILLIAM: What's it all for, Tom? What do you think you're going
to achieve?
TOM: I would have thought that was obvious.
WILLIAM: Not to me.
TOM: Scarlett, Eliza and the baby.
WILLIAM: Half of Scarlett, half Eliza, half a baby. Why are you
doing it? Out of some distorted sense of territoriality?
TOM: Is that all you think of me?
WILLIAM: I don't know what to think. You were always thoughtless
but never spiteful.
TOM: It's not spite.
WILLIAM: Then what? Pride, bravado, stupidity?
TOM: Why is it stupid to want my children and to do something
about it?
WILLIAM: Because you're going to lose!

Beat.

You're going to lose—and you're going to lay waste everything
in the process.
TOM: It's blackmail.
WILLIAM: I'm a private person, Tom. It was enough of a nightmare
the first time.

Tom: What are you saying—you'll take an overdose?

William: I'm trying to get it through your thick head—your thick heart—what it would do to me to have that dragged up again!

> Tom *looks at him, stricken.*

Tom: Don't make it a choice, don't make me choose!

> *Silence.*

I can't! I can't give it up! I can't give them up!

> *Pause.*

William: Then you'd better give me up.

> *Beat.*

I don't think you've got much chance of winning, but you can change that to no chance if you're still living with me. When they play their trump card in court, the only defence you'll have is that we're no longer together.

> Tom *gazes at him, stunned.*

Tom: That's not what you want. You don't want that.

William: You needn't worry about money. We'll sort something out. We've been together a long time.

Tom: William—

William: It's late, Tom. I've got to get up early.

> William *heads for the door.*

Tom: I don't want to leave you! I can't lose you!

> *He is crying.* William *is struck, turns back. But* Tom *is in a desperate bind.*

And I can't give up the kids!

> William *can only watch—*

I can't . . . I can't . . .

> *—as* Tom *melts down . . .*

I can't.

> *Lights down.*

Inter-scene images: high-rise view through the window of William's law office.

Scene 10: William's Office

WILLIAM *is holding* JESS.

JESS: I'm sorry! *She pulls back slightly, wipes at her eyes.* There's probably people waiting to see you.

WILLIAM: They can wait. Jess, it's so good to see you.

JESS: How can you be so nice?

WILLIAM: All I am is middle-aged. Though some say I was that even as a child.

JESS: I was terrified you'd—I don't know, scream at me. Throw me out.

WILLIAM: Sit down. Both of you.

> JESS *sits on the couch,* WILLIAM *sits beside her holding her hand.*

JESS: It would never have occurred to me. I want you to believe that.

WILLIAM: I know.

JESS: I wish I'd never said anything to Maeve. But it was years ago. I never thought.

WILLIAM: Of course you didn't.

JESS: Honestly, the only reason I would have told her was because it sounded so terrible for you.

WILLIAM: Jess—it's all right.

JESS: I mean, what happened—afterwards.

WILLIAM: I was a silly adolescent who overreacted. I had a brief period when I was seventeen of not being middle-aged— and it cured me for good.

JESS: You could have died.

WILLIAM: But I didn't. Pills are very imprecise like that. It was all very Tea and Sympathy.

> JESS *looks blank.*

A film. Before your time. Look, the boy was a total trollop—

which was apparent to everyone but his family. When they found out what had been going on after school in the orchestra room they cried rape and perversion, I was interviewed by burly policemen, my mother went screaming round the house with the vapours—I decided a bottle of her Mogadon might be the go. It wasn't. Instead I took up contract law—much the same effect.

JESS: Maeve's not very good when she feels threatened.

WILLIAM: It's not a situation that brings out the best in anyone. Except perhaps your lawyer.

JESS: You know Perry?

WILLIAM: Saw him in action in court once. Impressive. How's Scarlett?

JESS: Fine. She's . . . She keeps asking when she's going to go to your house.

WILLIAM: Little Miss Scarlett.

JESS: You know how much she loves you.

> WILLIAM *struggles with his emotion.*

WILLIAM: Tom's like a lost thing without them. It's tearing him up not being able to see them. With Eliza's birthday coming up—

JESS: Then tell him to stop! Just tell him—to stop!

WILLIAM: Darling, I have told him.

JESS: Why is he doing this? If he could see the hurt he's causing.

> *She collects herself.* WILLIAM *sees she's at the end of her tether.*

I shouldn't be here. I'm taking up your time.

WILLIAM: How are you holding up, Jess? Really.

JESS: I'm fine.

WILLIAM: Fine?

> JESS *nods miserably.*

Just dandy? Full of beans? On top of the world?

JESS, *nodding*: A box of fluffy ducks!

WILLIAM: Cuntful of dinghies!

JESS: What?

WILLIAM: I don't know. I knew this man who every time you said a box of birds he'd say a cuntful of dinghies! I never really understood it.

They look at each other, and start laughing. Jess *bursts into tears, laughing and crying at the same time.* William *rubs her back till she recovers.*

Jess: What am I going to do, William?

William: Well—I expect you're not going dancing all night.

Jess: Maeve blames me, I blame her . . . She says Scarlett has to change schools.

William: Because of the commute?

Jess, *nodding*: We have to get up early to walk to the station. Catch the train—then a bus.

William: The train? Where's the car?

> Jess *looks at him.*

Sold.

Jess: By the end of the week Scarlett's exhausted. I'm exhausted. It's not worth going back out so I usually stay in town during the day.

William: Doing what?

Jess, *shrugging*: Going to the Art Gallery, visiting, looking at things for the baby I can't afford to buy.

William: I want you to have something.

> He goes to his desk.

Jess: No.

> He comes back with a bankcard.

William: When Maeve cancelled the payment I redirected it into a new account. It's all in there.

> He places the card beside her.

I'll write out the PIN for you.

Jess: I can't take this.

William: You need a car. With everything else turning upside down in her life, Scarlett deserves to at least stay in the school she's happy at.

> He pushes the card an inch towards her.

Tell Maeve you sold a drawing, came into some money from a great aunt.

Jess *stares at the card.*

JESS: I was looking in a shop window at a weather-clock—with
   the little man and the woman. When the man comes out,
   the woman goes in. He's out in his coat making money, while
   she's inside raising all the weather-clock children. And for
   the first time I got it. I saw the point. Fair exchange, no
   robbery. *She looks up slowly.* I'm sorry, William. *She pushes
   the card back towards him.* It's not right for you to pay for me
   and my kids. When you don't get anything back for it.
WILLIAM: I love them.
JESS: From me. I don't do anything to deserve it.
WILLIAM: I've got some washing you could take home. Roll up
   your sleeves, boil up the copper.

   But JESS *is not playing.*

   Jess, what else can you do? You can't keep on like this. Can
   you?

   JESS *shakes her head.*

   Something has to be done. And Maeve's not in a position,
   you're not—
JESS: Perry is.
WILLIAM: Perry?
JESS: I shouldn't be talking to you. I shouldn't be here. But there's
   no one else I can. *She looks at him in fear.* I told Maeve not to
   get a lawyer.

   WILLIAM *stares at her for a moment, till light starts to dawn.*

WILLIAM: What's been going on, Jess?

   JESS *bites her lip.*

JESS: There were meetings with Perry. Maeve was always working.
   He started taking me to lunch. It was a break for me—I
   looked forward to it. We just started to talk. I told him all
   about Tom, Maeve, the great plan. He didn't say a thing—
   just let me go on. And I heard myself. For the first time I
   listened to myself trying to explain my life. And it was—
   laughable. How could I have believed any of it? How could
   I have ever thought it would work?

Who was it talking, even? Not me. It was this picture of myself I've held onto, always seeing myself as so free—not lesbian, not het—better than both. I could love anybody in the world, and no one could classify me, I couldn't be pinned down.

Then I looked at myself. Eight months pregnant, sitting in a restaurant I'd never be able to afford, ordering a third coffee, desperate for another fifteen minutes before I had to go back out to my life. Because all of a sudden the music's stopped. And there's only one chair left. But it's the chair labelled poor, labelled lesbian, labelled Epuni station at 7:40 every morning. And I can't sit in that chair. I can't stand it, William. I hate myself for it, but I can't live with that lack of—light.

WILLIAM: So you had another coffee.

JESS: He's smart and he's funny, and he's kind.

WILLIAM: And don't tell me—he loves children. Jess, what are you doing?

JESS: I don't know! I don't know what to do! I just know I've made a mess. I've fucked it all up!

WILLIAM: Not yet.

JESS: From the beginning!

WILLIAM: Jess—listen—apart from anything else, what Perry's doing is unethical. Lawyer and client—he's risking every-thing—he could be struck off.

JESS *pulls back.*

JESS: I shouldn't have told you. *She gets up.*

WILLIAM: That's not what I mean—I'm not going to use the information—for God's sake, Jess!

JESS: I've got to go.

WILLIAM, *proffering the bankcard*: Jess, take the card. Don't get rushed into anything.

JESS *just looks at him and exits.*

WILLIAM: Jess!

Lights down.

Inter-scene images: Restaurant—coffee cups half-drunk. Street outside school—Tom walking off with Scarlett and Eliza.

Scene 11: Maeve and Jess's flat

MAEVE, *very agitated, is pacing back and forth on the phone. She holds something tightly clenched in her left hand.*

MAEVE: Well, what are you doing? I want you to tell me what you're doing.

> *Beat.*

> Of course I have—everyone I can think of. I've told you every place! I don't have a car!

> WILLIAM *rushes in, looking white and stressed.*

> I'll be here. *She hangs up.*

WILLIAM: He won't hurt them.

> MAEVE *doesn't reply.*

> You know that, Maeve. I've been home, there's no sign, but if we just sit tight—

MAEVE: I've called the police.

WILLIAM: I told you—[there's no need]

MAEVE: You don't tell me anything! You don't pay for this house! You're nobody's father here!

> *They stare at each other.*

WILLIAM: Let's just draw breath, take it easy.

MAEVE: I don't know what's happening to the girls!

WILLIAM: Nothing's happening to them. Or do you think Tom's a child molester as well?

MAEVE: What did he say to you?

WILLIAM: Nothing.

MAEVE: He must have!

WILLIAM: Oh no, that's right—over breakfast he did mention something about abducting his daughters!

MAEVE *turns away.*

MAEVE: I should never have put Eliza in daycare. That stupid woman! How could she just let Tom walk off with her!

WILLIAM: He's a charmer—you have to give him that.

> Some of MAEVE's *distress shows through as she unclenches her left hand, revealing Eliza's scrunched-up jingle-ball. She presses it to her face and breathes in its smell.* WILLIAM *reaches out to comfort her—*

Maeve . . .

> MAEVE *fends him off, escaping.*

MAEVE: Where's Jess?

WILLIAM: You still haven't heard from her?

MAEVE: She should have been home hours ago.

> MAEVE *paces.*

Scarlett was supposed to be going to a friend's house, it's the one day Jess didn't have to do the school pick up. She was seeing the midwife this morning, said she'd have lunch in town . . .

WILLIAM: She's just off the radar. Shopping.

MAEVE: She's got no money!

WILLIAM: Gone for a swim then. Anything.

MAEVE: Jess couldn't be with Tom as well?

WILLIAM: No.

> MAEVE *stares at him.*

MAEVE: If they're all together, the police are looking for the wrong thing—not a couple with children. They could go right past them.

WILLIAM: Jess won't be with Tom.

MAEVE: I'm going to report her missing.

> MAEVE *picks up the phone.*

WILLIAM: Maeve—no.

MAEVE: She didn't tell me she was going anywhere—it doesn't make sense!

She dials. WILLIAM *watches her.*

WILLIAM: I might know where she is.

    MAEVE *stops.*

MAEVE: Where?
WILLIAM: I don't have the number.
MAEVE: Where?
WILLIAM: You've got the number.

    MAEVE *stares at him. As she goes to speak, the front door bangs (off).* JESS *comes in. She stops, seeing* MAEVE *and* WILLIAM.

MAEVE: Where have you been?
JESS, *warily*: William . . .
WILLIAM: Tom's got Scarlett and Eliza.
JESS, *taking a moment to register*: 'Got'?
WILLIAM: He picked them up from school and daycare.
JESS: Scarlett's staying with a friend. She's having a sleepover.
MAEVE: Tom got to school first. He picked her up—he already had Eliza. I've been trying to call you for hours.

    JESS *goes pale.*

JESS: What's he doing, William?
WILLIAM: I'm sure he'll be home with them—shortly.
JESS: He's not at your house?

    WILLIAM *shakes his head.*

He's taking them.
WILLIAM: You don't know that.
JESS: He's going to leave the country with them.
MAEVE: They haven't got passports.
JESS: He could smuggle them out.
WILLIAM: Of course not.
JESS: Then what? What's he trying to do?

    Beat.

You don't think he'd—
WILLIAM: No.
JESS: You hear about it all the time. That guy up north and his kids—in the car.

Maeve: No.

Jess: How's he been?

> William *looks at her.*

William: Under a bit of stress actually.

Jess: You know what I mean!

William: If you think he would harm those girls in any way—

Jess: What do you call kidnapping them?

William: He hasn't kidnapped them!

Jess: I'm going to phone the police.

Maeve: I've already called them.

> Jess *looks at her.*

They've been here and got the details. They're looking for them.

> Jess *sinks down in a chair.*

Jess: He couldn't hurt Scarlett—no matter what he thinks of me.

William: He wouldn't hurt either of them. He just wants to see his children. It killed him not being able to see Eliza on her birthday. He bought her a present. That's what it'll be about.

Jess: No one's stopping him from seeing them.

William: As long as he gives up his claim to them.

Jess: I didn't want it to come to this. To court.

William: No, you just wanted him to grin and bear it—or rather grin while you bear it. And raise it.

Maeve, *to* William: I think you should go.

William: Where?

Maeve: Home. Tom's more likely to go there than here.

William: I've left messages.

Maeve: This doesn't concern you.

William: Concern? I'm concerned to my wits end! I get up in the morning and I feel like I'm going to puke!

Maeve: Why do you always have to push yourself into the middle of everything?

Jess: Where are they? Where is she? What's he doing?

Maeve: Calm down. You'll do something to the baby.

Jess, *struggling up*: I can't stand this!

Maeve: For God's sake sit down. *To* William. Please.

WILLIAM: That's right, Jess—you're holding the trump card there. If Jess can't stand it then the whole world has to stop.

MAEVE: She's not the one snatching kids!

WILLIAM: Isn't she holding one for ransom right there?

JESS: No!

WILLIAM: As if that's not enough—you have to bring up this business of mine—make him choose between hurting me and hurting himself.

JESS: That wasn't me—I told you that.

> MAEVE *gazes coolly at* JESS.

MAEVE: When was this?

WILLIAM: You want to know how he's been? A bloody mess! *Sophie's Choice* is how he's been! Because he loves his children, and he loves me. And you're using that as a gun at his head. He's just a boy! You've pushed him and pushed him and pushed him—till now you've got what you wanted.

MAEVE: How is this what we wanted?

JESS: I just want them back.

WILLIAM: Then clap your hands and shout hooray!

> *They stare at him.*

You can't abduct kids then expect to get custody. He's made going to court a complete waste of time. It's over.

> *Beat.*

And once he understands that—he's going to fall apart. And just how am I supposed to put him back together?

> *Emotion starts to leak through.*

You want me to go home? Why would he go there? What have I got to offer him? Half-painted clouds on a wall.

> MAEVE *is struck by his vulnerability. She reaches out a hand.*

MAEVE: William . . .

JESS: What if he realises now? What's that going to make him do?

WILLIAM: Just for one second see who is hurt here, Jess.

JESS: He's taken my child.

WILLIAM: You want her home?

JESS: Yes!

WILLIAM: But can you make up your mind where that home is?

MAEVE: What?

WILLIAM: It's not too late, Jess. Steer for once, don't just let yourself drift.

> JESS *looks at him.*

MAEVE: Is everyone talking in another language?

> *They freeze as they hear the front door open—then the sound of the girls' voices.* MAEVE *and* JESS *head for the door.* WILLIAM *holds* JESS *back.*

WILLIAM: Don't frighten them.

> MAEVE *exits.* JESS *pushes* WILLIAM *away and goes to follow.* TOM *comes in the door. He and* JESS *are face to face. They stare at each other.* JESS *hits* TOM *across the face with all her force. She exits. She and* MAEVE *can be heard talking to the girls, particularly an excited Scarlett.* WILLIAM *and* TOM *look at each other,* WILLIAM *makes a move towards him but* TOM *evades.*
>
> *Pause.*

Got the time on yer, cock?

> *No answer.* WILLIAM *steps up behind* TOM, *puts his arms round him.*

What's this thing called, love?

> *No answer.* WILLIAM *leans forward to lay his face alongside* TOM'*s, eyes closed.*

Where've you been? Eh?

TOM, *slowly*: I didn't want to be a McDonald's dad. So we went one up. To Valentines. You can put your own chocolate sauce on there. You don't even have to have anything to put it on.

Then I didn't know what to do. They'd played and come back. I took them to play some more. I couldn't think of where to go. It was filling up for dinner. Eliza flew at another kid—then started to scream the place down. I went to pick her up. She bit me. Right through my shirt.

He touches his shirt above his waist, traces of dried blood.

Drew blood.

WILLIAM: Baby.

TOM: No. She's the baby. They're the babies.

He turns to face WILLIAM.

I've blown it, haven't I?

WILLIAM: You'd blown it before you started.

MAEVE *comes back in.*

MAEVE: Jess has got them upstairs. *She picks up the phone.* I'm calling the police to say they've been found. If you don't leave now I'll tell them to come round.

TOM: What's wrong with Eliza?

MAEVE: Besides you kidnapping her?

TOM: She just glazed over—like I wasn't there.

MAEVE: It's a bit late for you to try to impress me with your fatherhood skills.

TOM: I'm worried about her.

MAEVE: At least you knew where she was.

TOM: She's never been like this.

MAEVE *snaps.*

MAEVE: There's nothing wrong with her!

WILLIAM: Come on, Tom. Let's go home.

MAEVE *dials.* TOM *watches her. She ignores him.*

MAEVE, *on the phone*: Hello. I reported two girls missing earlier. Eliza and Scarlett. Yes, they're fine.

Beat.

He brought them back.

She holds the phone and stares at TOM *and* WILLIAM *challengingly.*

WILLIAM: Tom.

He leads TOM *out.* MAEVE *watches them go.*

MAEVE, *on the phone*: Yes. Yes, I'm here.

> *The sound of the front door closing is heard.*

> No, we just want to leave it there. Thank you for your help.

> *She hangs up. She bites her lip.* JESS *comes in.*

JESS: That's it. That's absolutely it now.

> *She reaches out to touch* MAEVE. MAEVE *looks at her.*

MAEVE: Where were you?

> *Lights down.*

Inter-scene images: A medical referral letter to 'Parents of Eliza'.

Scene 12: Maeve and Jess's flat

A month later. MAEVE *lights a candle, pours two glasses of sparkling grape juice. She looks at the specialist's letter with sadness and fear, before shoving it down the couch as she hears* JESS *coming.* JESS, *now at full term, enters, sees the glasses and candle and stops.*

JESS: Oh.

> *There is a moment of awkwardness.*

I thought you'd have—
MAEVE: Forgotten?
JESS: Let it go past. Like I was going to.
MAEVE: It's a tradition. Due date, no baby—you get a present.

> *She holds out a small wrapped gift.* JESS *takes it and stares at it.*

There hasn't been much time lately—
JESS: I know.

> *Beat.*

I have to lie down.

MAEVE, *proffering the drink*: Grape juice?

JESS: No. Thanks. It gives me reflux. You have yours.

> *She lowers herself onto the couch.* MAEVE *sips her grape juice.*

MAEVE: I just wanted to try—

JESS, *interrupting*: Well don't. Don't try so hard. It just makes me feel worse.

> *She puts a hand over her eyes, stressed.*

Sorry.

MAEVE: To remind you—that this is us.

> JESS *nods.*

Here. The two of us. The girls asleep . . .

JESS: I just can't think straight right now. I can't take any more pressure.

MAEVE: I'm not trying to pressure you.

JESS: I don't know why everything has to be so much of a struggle! I should only have to worry about one thing—getting this baby out happy and healthy.

MAEVE: That is all you've got to worry about. We're safe now. The case is dropped. This is where we wanted to be.

> JESS *looks at her.*

Open it.

> JESS *looks at the gift and slowly unwraps it. It's a voucher for . . .*

JESS: Aquacise.

MAEVE: In case you go another couple of weeks. You can spend every morning in the pool if you want.

JESS: You said we couldn't afford it.

MAEVE: I sold some books. None of yours.

> JESS *is silent.*

If you don't get to use it much before the baby comes we can get a refund.

JESS: You checked?

MAEVE: Mmmm.

JESS: You see, I couldn't do that. I couldn't buy a voucher for something and ask if I could get my money back. Scrabbling around for every little piece of money.

> MAEVE *feels the barb.*

It's a fault of mine—I know it is. I wish I could be like you.

MAEVE: I want to feel like I can make my own way—that I'm not dependent on anyone.

JESS: I always liked that about you. I was attracted to it. It just starts to look like a luxury when we've both got other people dependent on us.

> MAEVE *is silent.*

It's just another sort of pride, isn't it? Ego. And what good's that if the kids are deprived of the support they need.

MAEVE: We support them.

JESS: There's all kinds of support.

MAEVE: What kind of support did you see him giving you?

JESS: I don't want to talk about Perry.

MAEVE: Neither do I. I just want to forget about him, and him and you. Stop—seeing it.

JESS: I've said and said I'm sorry.

MAEVE: I thought—with him out of our lives, you proming you wouldn't see him, talk to him—I could start to get over it. *We* could. Together.

> JESS *is silent. The moment gapes.*

Jess.

> JESS *looks up slowly.*

Tell me you want me.

JESS: I don't want to hurt you.

MAEVE: Please.

JESS: I told you—I'm confused.

MAEVE: What do you want?

JESS: I don't know. I don't know what I want.

MAEVE: Tell me what you want!

JESS: I don't know!

MAEVE: Who are you? Are you gay? Or straight?
JESS: It's not as easy as that.
MAEVE: It's perfectly easy for someone who knows who they are!

> *Beat.* MAEVE *turns away.*

JESS: I don't know why you can't see how hard this is for me.
MAEVE: Why? Because you love me?
JESS: For one thing.

> MAEVE *looks at her.*

That goes without saying.
MAEVE: Certainly has the last few months. And love-making.
JESS: Well look at me.
MAEVE: What did you do with him?

> JESS *looks up.*

Oh, I'm sure he wouldn't have taken the risk of penetration bringing you on prematurely. But there's plenty of other things. Did you touch his cock?
JESS: Just don't.
MAEVE: To see whether you liked it? Whether you could make the switch? Did you suck it? Did you suck his cock—is that what you did?
JESS: That's enough!
MAEVE: Oh no, I bet he was the perfect gentleman. Never laid a finger on you. While all the time wondering how long you'd take to tighten up after you squeeze that baby out.
JESS: Yes, I liked it with him! I liked it with Tom! I liked it with every man! Is that what you want me to say?
MAEVE: Is it the truth?

> *Beat.*

JESS: Yes.

> MAEVE *stares at her, broken.*

And I liked it with you.

> *She reaches out, but* MAEVE *turns away.*

It's not about sex, Maeve. It's not just you and me I have to think about. It's the kids.

MAEVE: That's easy—we're a family, we need to be together.

JESS: I want it to be that simple. But it's not.

MAEVE: It's never you, is it? It's never what you want, Jess. You've always got to have somebody to hide behind. How can you talk about what's good for the kids while you're sitting there thinking about splitting them up?

JESS, *quietly*: Because that might be what they need.

> MAEVE *stares at her.*

It can't go on like it is, Maeve. Scarlett doesn't even want to come home any more.

> MAEVE *doesn't reply.*

Eliza's got to stop lashing out—she's going to really hurt her! And what's she going to do to the baby if I don't watch her every second?

MAEVE: That's what you mean when you say the kids. Your kids. What about what's best for Eliza?

JESS: I love Eliza. But she can't be happy like this either. Look at what she's doing—the tantrums, withdrawals, she hardly speaks.

MAEVE: Why are you saying this now? What are you trying to do?

JESS: I'm trying to tell you something has to change.

MAEVE: Or she loses her sister? She's had Scarlett all her life.

JESS: Scarlett doesn't want to go anywhere near her. She's afraid of her!

MAEVE: It's not her fault!

JESS: It's not Scarlett's fault! Or mine!

MAEVE: But it's mine?

JESS: As long as you won't even admit there's a problem . . .

MAEVE: I know there's a problem!

JESS: But you don't *do* anything!

> Beat.

MAEVE: So it has to get better. Eliza's behaviour has to get better— or you, Scarlett and the baby are up and off, is that it?

> JESS *doesn't reply.*

What if she gets worse, Jess? What then?

JESS: That's ridiculous.

MAEVE: What if she does?

JESS: The only reason her behaviour would get any worse is if you
keep ignoring it.

MAEVE: What if she just—gets worse—and worse?

> JESS *is looking for something.*

JESS: Look—I've got a book on behavioural problems in children.
It's a new method for dealing with tantrums, biting,
screaming fits . . .

MAEVE: Jess . . .

> MAEVE *reaches into the couch to retrieve the letter.*

JESS: It hasn't even been published here—it was on Amazon.

> MAEVE *freezes at this.* JESS *finds the book and turns back to
> hand it to* MAEVE. MAEVE *just stares at her.*

MAEVE: Where did you get it?

> *Beat.*

JESS: Perry ordered it for me.

> *There is a frozen moment.*

I know what I said. I know! We just met for coffee.

> *She is still proffering the book.*

You need something, Maeve. We need something. What does
it matter where it comes from?

MAEVE: You talked to him about Eliza.

JESS: He's seen the marks on Scarlett. He wants to help.

> MAEVE *takes the book—and throws it hard at* JESS. MAEVE
> *and* JESS *stare at each other.*

> *Lights down.*

Inter-scene images: Maeve walking with Eliza.

Scene 13: Café

WILLIAM *and* TOM *are having Sunday brunch.* WILLIAM *is reading the paper;* TOM *is tearing a paper napkin into neat strips.*

WILLIAM: What would you say to Berlin?

TOM: Gutentag?

WILLIAM: Ach—sie sprechen Deutsch! Sehr gut!

TOM: Que?

WILLIAM, *singing:* Come to the Cabaret, old chum . . . Sally Bowles, Checkpoint Charlie, biggest building site in the world . . .

TOM: Sure.

> WILLIAM *watches* TOM *for a moment.*

WILLIAM: I can see where she gets it from.

> TOM *looks up,* WILLIAM *indicates the strips.*

Eliza. *He folds his paper.* Or do you prefer the Cinque Terre?

TOM: What?

WILLIAM: Il mio amico—se non siete stati a Cinque Terre che non avete vissuto!

TOM: Will you stop talking to me in other languages! I know you know them.

WILLIAM: English it is then.

TOM: It's just a bit early for me.

WILLIAM: If I didn't get you up you wouldn't emerge till three in the afternoon.

> *Beat.*

TOM: What is it then? Chinky whatever it was.

WILLIAM: Five villages—you walk between them. Look Tom, if you don't want to go—

TOM: You'll go by yourself?

WILLIAM: The idea is to take you away.

TOM: You love it. You're like some dowager duchess out of a Merchant-Ivory film with your travelling companion. What'd you used to do before I came along?

WILLIAM: Dream.

> *Beat.*

I love you baby.

Beat.

Sometimes I think I'll come home and the house will be empty. Just me again.

Tom: Give you a break from all the drama.

William: I couldn't face that. Tom.

Tom: You face everything.

Beat.

William: We could always go back to Greece.

Tom: She could be in labour right now.

William: We would have heard.

Tom: Would we?

WILLIAM *has no answer. He looks round.*

William: How long does it take to make an eggs bene?

Tom: William?

William: Hmm?

Tom: What am I going to do with my life?

They stare at each other.

Lights down.

Audio of labour and birth accompany inter-scene images: photographs of Jess in the hospital in labour (taken by Perry)—Scarlett is there—culminating in the birth of the baby. The last is one Perry has got the midwife to take of Jess, Scarlett, the baby and him together.

The final image is the birth notice in the paper: Jess and Perry announce the arrival of Jacob . . .

The audio fades to a rhythmic thudding of Eliza kicking the wall.

Scene 14: Maeve's flat

MAEVE *sits on the couch staring blankly, holding scissors—and two strips of newspaper containing the bisected birth notice. Eliza is kicking the wall in the next room.* MAEVE *is at the limit of what she can take. Eliza's kicking starts to get to her.*

MAEVE: No! I said no—I'm keeping them!

> *The sound of Eliza kicking the wall continues.*

Stop it! STOP IT!

> MAEVE *gets up—holding the scissors—and goes out.*

Off stage: Look what you've done! Let go! No! NO!

> *Eliza abruptly starts to scream, and keeps screaming.* MAEVE *comes back into the room, ashen. She slumps down on the couch, clutching the scissors (now open) in her fist. She stares at them—they're red with blood.*
>
> *Through Eliza's screams comes the sound of knocking at the front door.* MAEVE *doesn't seem to hear it.*

TOM, *off:* Maeve?

> *More knocking.*

Maeve!

> TOM *bursts in, drawn by Eliza's screams.*

Maeve! What's . . . ?

> MAEVE *doesn't look up.* TOM *sees the blood oozing through her clenched fingers.*

Maeve?

> *He looks towards the sound of Eliza screaming and quickly exits. The screams rise, fall, abate—then stop. After a moment* TOM *comes back. Moving to* MAEVE, *he gently opens her fingers, removes the scissors and inspects the cut across her fingers.*
>
> MAEVE *seems to notice him for the first time. She goes to pull her hand back but* TOM *holds on.*

Here.

He fishes out his handkerchief, wraps it round her hand and gently folds the fingers back over.

I let her go under the bed. Pulled out all that stuff you'd packed under there.

MAEVE, *hardly there*: She has to learn.

TOM *picks up the two strips of birth notice and fits them together.*

TOM: 'Jacob'. Could be worse. Perry Junior for instance.

MAEVE *doesn't react.*

You didn't really want to keep this did you, Maeve?

MAEVE *doesn't reply.*

How about we split it? Fifty:fifty.

He proffers a strip to her. Slowly MAEVE *looks at him.*

MAEVE, *almost to herself*: She hasn't asked where Scarlett's gone, or Jess. She doesn't miss them. I could die and she wouldn't know or care. But take the scissors off her, move the furniture . . .

TOM: It's not her fault.

MAEVE: Go away, Tom.

TOM: I know you don't want me here, but listen to me.

MAEVE: Just go.

TOM: I found something. *He takes a book from his pocket.* She's in here, Maeve. Everything about Eliza is in this book. The obsessions, the tantrums . . .

MAEVE *doesn't even glance at it.*

I couldn't understand why she seemed to be going backwards—her speech, the way she is with other kids. Until I read this. I think I know what's going on with her.

MAEVE *reaches down behind the cushions of the couch and pulls out the specialist's letter. She hands it to* TOM—*who, puzzled, glances over it. He's stunned, struck to the heart by the stark reality.*

Maeve: Got your answer? Happy now?

Tom: This is a month old. Why didn't you tell me?

> Maeve *is silent.*

Does Jess know? Why not?

Maeve: I knew she'd leave. She'd agonise, she'd wring her hands. But for Scarlett, for the sake of the baby . . .

> *She's beginning to come slowly to the surface.*

She's gone anyway. But I still can't say it. Can't speak the word out loud.

> *Beat.*

Every day I've watched her getting further and further away. Sinking. I've got my arms out to catch her but she just keeps falling. I've kept her safe from everything outside—cot death, cars, strangers. Now for this to come—inside her. It's a punishment.

Tom: No.

Maeve: I wanted her to be better than me. Not awkward, at odds with everyone. Not alone.

Tom: She's not alone.

Maeve: That's what I loved so much about Jess. How everything comes to her so easily. I was desperate to be part of that ease for once, to be warm in the sunlight. Trouble is—you stand there and it shows up every shadow. Like a spotlight on me. And on Eliza. Prickly Maeve and her difficult daughter, hobbling along behind. Like it's a club foot I've passed on.

Tom: Maeve—

Maeve: Because I wanted too much. Because I wanted her to be like Scarlett who everyone just loves best.

Tom: Not me.

Maeve: All of you.

Tom: Why do you have to try to do everything by yourself?

Maeve: She's my daughter—

Tom: Would it kill you to let me in?

Maeve: She's my daughter.

Tom: What do I have to do—marry you? Fine!

Maeve: Go home, Tom. Go home to William.

'You Can't Always Get What You Want' plays. On the other side of the stage WILLIAM *hurries into his house.*

WILLIAM: Only me!

By the music playing, he thinks TOM *is there.*

Tom, are you packed? Tom?

No answer. WILLIAM *picks up the stereo remote to turn the music off. There's a note underneath it. He knows what it is before he reads it.*

TOM, *to* MAEVE: You were right. I had to grow up. I couldn't do that with William.

After glancing over the note, WILLIAM *tears it slowly in half and sags into a chair.*

TOM: You can't do it all, Maeve.

MAEVE: I'll get help.

TOM: I'm here! I'm the only person you can ever get who feels anything like you do about her!

The jingle-ball rolls out onto stage. After a moment ELIZA *follows and picks it up.*

She's my bone, my blood.

TOM *crosses and lifts* ELIZA *into his arms. She shows no response as he holds her to him.*

She doesn't belong to me. Or you. We belong to her.

MAEVE *looks at them. She's crumbling.*

MAEVE: I could have hurt her. I could have really hurt her. Even though I know she's . . . she's—

TOM: Autistic.

MAEVE: Autistic.

And with the saying of the word comes the wave of grief
MAEVE *has been holding back.* TOM *cradles* ELIZA *as* MAEVE
sobs convulsively.

TOM *lets her grieve.* MAEVE *stretches out her arms.* TOM
brings ELIZA *to* MAEVE *and wraps them both in his arms,*
holding them.

After a while, MAEVE *starts to laugh through her tears.*
TOM *looks at her.*

TOM: What?
MAEVE: You proposed to me.
TOM: Did not.
MAEVE: Did so! *She shakes her head.* Me and you.
TOM: You've got to laugh, don't you?

Images of clouds and blue sky move across the set and the characters.

WILLIAM *hauls himself to his feet and turns the music up loud as it*
reaches the 'get what you need' part of the song. He starts to dance
madly, losing himself in the music as it soars up into the choral climax
of the song.

Lights fade—on TOM, MAEVE *and* ELIZA *first;* WILLIAM *last, as he*
carries on dancing.